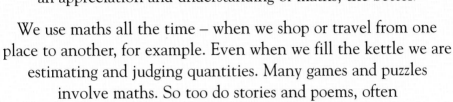

Maths Together

There's a lot more to maths than number: it's an important language which helps us describe explain the world we live in. So the earlier children develop an appreciation and understanding of maths, the better.

We use maths all the time – when we shop or travel from one place to another, for example. Even when we fill the kettle we are estimating and judging quantities. Many games and puzzles involve maths. So too do stories and poems, often in an imaginative and interesting way.

Maths Together is a collection of high-quality picture books designed to introduce children, simply and enjoyably, to basic mathematical ideas – from counting and measuring to pattern and probability. By listening to the stories and rhymes, talking about them and asking questions, children will gain the confidence to try out the mathematical ideas for themselves – an important step in their numeracy development.

You don't have to be a mathematician to help your child learn maths. Just as by reading aloud you play a vital role in their literacy development, so by sharing the *Maths Together* books with your child, you will play an important part in developing their understanding of mathematics. To help you, each book has detailed notes at the back, explaining the mathematical ideas that it introduces, with suggestions for further related activities.

With *Maths Together*, you can count on doing the very best for your child.

For Milo
E.B.

For Helen Craig
D.P.

First published 1993 by Walker Books Ltd
87 Vauxhall Walk, London SE11 5HJ

This edition published 1999

2 4 6 8 10 9 7 5 3 1

Text © 1993 Eileen Browne
Illustrations © 1993 David Parkins
Introductory and concluding notes
© 1999 Jeannie Billington and Grace Cook

Printed in Singapore

British Library Cataloguing in Publication Data
A catalogue record for this book is
available from the British Library.

ISBN 0-7445-6835-8 (hb)
ISBN 0-7445-6806-4 (pb)

No Problem

Eileen Browne • David Parkins

WALKER BOOKS

AND SUBSIDIARIES

LONDON • BOSTON • SYDNEY

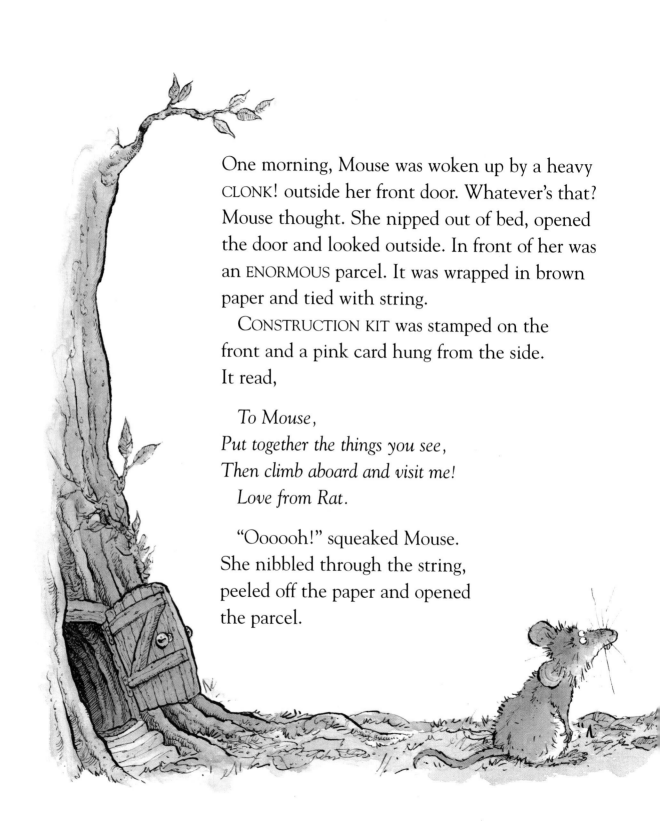

One morning, Mouse was woken up by a heavy
CLONK! outside her front door. Whatever's that?
Mouse thought. She nipped out of bed, opened
the door and looked outside. In front of her was
an ENORMOUS parcel. It was wrapped in brown
paper and tied with string.

CONSTRUCTION KIT was stamped on the
front and a pink card hung from the side.
It read,

> To Mouse,
> *Put together the things you see,*
> *Then climb aboard and visit me!*
> *Love from Rat.*

"Oooooh!" squeaked Mouse.
She nibbled through the string,
peeled off the paper and opened
the parcel.

Inside was a mountain of bits and pieces –
just *waiting* to be put together.

Mouse sniffed them and snuffled them.
She poked them and prodded them.

"I can put these together," she said.
"No problem."

To Mouse,
Put together the things you see,
Then climb aboard and visit me!
Love from Rat

She was in such a hurry to begin that she forgot to look for the instructions. She didn't see the sheet of paper which said, CONSTRUCTION KIT. HOW TO PUT IT TOGETHER!

Mouse set to work.

She joined pipes here
and fixed wheels there.

She twisted
and turned things.

She fiddled
and twiddled things.

She bolted bolts
and tightened nuts.

Then she stepped back to see what she'd made.
"Cor!" said Mouse. "What *can* it be? It's a bit like a bike …
but it isn't a bike. I think I'll call it a Bikeoodle-Doodle."
    She climbed on, started the engine and set off to see Rat.

The Bikeoodle-Doodle was very jumpy and very wobbly. It kept going on to one wheel and doing "wheelies" by mistake.

"Ooooh!" cried Mouse, hanging on tight. "PerHAPS I haven't put it toGETHER quite riGHT."

She was tottering along on one wheel, when she met Badger.

"Well, hello there, Mouse," growled Badger, peering over the top of her glasses. "What is that very peculiar *thing* you're riding?"

"It's a Bikeoodle-Doodle," squeaked Mouse. "A construction kit. A present from Rat. I put it together, but it isn't quite right. It's very jumpy and very wobbly."

"Have you got the instructions?" asked Badger.

"No," said Mouse. "Can you help?"

Badger polished her glasses and blinked at the Bikeoodle-Doodle. "Well now," she mumbled. "Let's see. Hmmmmmm." Then she looked up and said, "I can fix this. No problem."

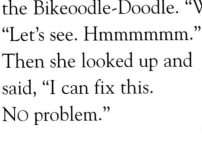

Badger unscrewed
the screws and
unbolted the bolts.

She shifted and
shoved things.

She changed and
rearranged things.

She reset the pipes and the wheels.

Then she stepped back to see what she'd made.

"Ahhh," said Badger. "What *can* it be? It's a bit like a car ... but it isn't a car. I think I'll call it a Jaloppy-Doppy."

"Come on," said Mouse. "Let's go to Rat's."

Mouse and Badger climbed in the Jaloppy-Doppy and set off to see Rat.

The Jaloppy-Doppy was very bumpy and very rattly, and not at all comfortable.

"Per-haps," said Badger, bouncing up and down, "I hav-en't put it to-ge-ther quite ri-ght."

They were juddering along a river bank, when they met Otter.

"Hey!" grinned Otter. "What the heck is that?"

"It's a Jaloppy-Doppy," snorted Badger. "A construction kit. Rat sent it to Mouse. I put it together, but it isn't quite right. It's very bumpy and very rattly."

"Got the instructions?" asked Otter.

"Sadly, no," said Badger. "Can you help?"

Otter dived into the Jaloppy-Doppy and rolled out again. She climbed up the front and slid down the back.

"I can fix this," said Otter. "No problem."

She squeezed underneath
and unbolted the bolts.

She switched bits
and swapped bits.

She flipped bits
and flopped bits.

She moved all the wheels and
she rebuilt the pipes.

Then she stepped back to see
what she'd made.

"Wow!" barked Otter. "What
can it be? It's a bit like a boat …
but it sure ain't a boat. I think I'll
call it a Boater-Roater."

"Come on, then," said Mouse
and Badger. "Let's go to Rat's."

Mouse, Badger and Otter pushed
the Boater-Roater on to the river.
They jumped in and set off
to see Rat.

The Boater-Roater kept rocking and rolling, and letting in lots of water.

"*Geeeee*," said Otter, swaying to and fro.

"Perha*aaaaaaps* I haven't put it toge*eeeee*ther quite r*iiiii*ight."

They were sailing round a bend, when they met Shrew.

"Hi!" piped Shrew. "What's that?"

"It's a Boater-Roater," said Otter. "A construction kit. Rat sent it to Mouse. I put it together, but it ain't quite right. It keeps rocking and rolling."

"Have you got the instructions?" asked Shrew.

"No," said Otter. "Can you help?"

Shrew jumped into the Boater-Roater and scampered all over it. She peeped in corners, peered through pipes and peeked round poles. Then … she found something.

"Yes!" said Shrew.
"I can fix this.
No problem."

They pulled the Boater-Roater on to the river bank.

Shrew didn't

She *completely dismantled* the Boater-Roater.

And peeping down

"Pass me this!" she ordered Mouse.

"Pass me that!" she snapped at Badger.

"Give me those!" she said to Otter.

switch bits, or swap bits, or flip bits, or flop bits.

at a sheet of paper, she laid all the pieces in rows on the grass.

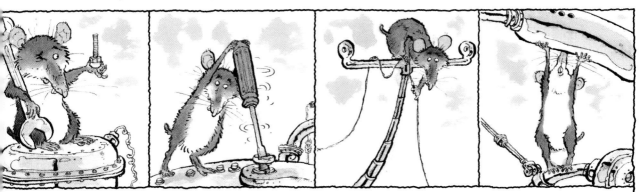

Then bit by bit and nut by bolt, she built a wonderful …

AEROPLANE!

"How did you do it?" asked Mouse, Badger and Otter.

"Easy!" laughed Shrew. "I followed the instructions!"
And she waved the sheet of paper that said,

CONSTRUCTION KIT.
HOW TO PUT IT TOGETHER!

"Well, I'll be blowed!" said the others. "Come on
then, let's go to Rat's."

So Mouse, Badger, Otter and Shrew climbed into the
aeroplane and set off to see Rat.

They raced across the grass and rose into the air.

"*Yoo-reeka!*" squeaked Mouse.

"*Yowler-rowler!*" growled Badger.

"*Bonanza!*" barked Otter.

"*Yazoo!*" piped Shrew.

The aeroplane didn't jump or wobble,
or bump or rattle, or rock or roll. It just flew
smoothly through the sky all the way to Rat's.

They landed the plane and climbed out.

"Look!" said Mouse. "There are balloons on Rat's door. She must be having a party."

The door swung open and out jumped Rat.

"*Happy birthday, Mouse!*" said Rat.

"Happy birthday," said Badger and Otter and Shrew. "Had you forgotten? It's your birthday! We're having a party."

"My birthday?" said Mouse. "Well, I never!"

"I see you got the aeroplane," said Rat. "Did you have any trouble putting it together?"

Mouse winked at Badger. Otter winked at Shrew.
"Of course not," they said. "No problem."

About this book

In *No Problem*, Mouse, Badger and Otter use
their knowledge of different machines (a bike, a boat,
a car) to fit the shapes of the construction kit together.
They do so by trial and error – estimating, thinking and
adjusting as they go along. They compare the machines
they've built to the ones they know, and realize
they haven't been put together correctly.

Shrew has a different, more systematic way.
She follows the instructions, checks all the pieces by
laying them out, and fits them together in order.
The problem of Mouse's present seems to be a big one,
but each animal breaks it down into manageable bits
and solves it in their own way.

At this stage, the particular way children
solve a problem is less important than their
willingness to try different ways and to share and
learn from them. As they gain confidence, they
learn to choose more efficient, appropriate
ways to tackle problems.

Notes for parents

Looking at the shape and size of parcels gives us an idea of what's inside. Use the picture of the parcel at the beginning of the story to talk about what Mouse's present could – and couldn't – be. Imagining different possibilities is a good way to help children learn about shapes.

First I put on my socks, then my shoes.

Everyday activities, like getting dressed, can show children that it's helpful to do things in a particular order.

I want to take my ball to Gran's.

Do you need anything else? What if it rains?

In *No Problem*, Shrew checks off the bits of the construction kit on a list. Whenever you talk about what they need to take on an outing, you are encouraging children to check things and organize their thoughts and ideas.

The animals in the story watch each other solving a problem in different ways. Children often see you tackling everyday tasks, and it can be helpful to explain what you're doing as you go along.

If you put it on its side, I can fit the nut.

Many children enjoy doing jigsaw puzzles. A jigsaw is a problem to be solved, and children often develop their own ways of approaching it. They may do the edges first, sort the pieces by colour, or look at the picture to get an idea of the whole. You can sometimes help by pointing out that shapes look different from different angles.

What if you turn it round?

It fits!

In the story, the animals look at the different shapes and decide how to fit them together.
Here are some useful mathematical words for talking about making things:

long	solid	slide	over	triangle
short	hollow	roll	through	cuboid
wide	curved	turn	inside	cone
narrow	flat	fit	same	hexagon
thick	round	match	way	edge
thin	straight	flip	opposite	corner

Like the animals in the book, your child might enjoy making their own version of a fantastic machine. They could use cardboard boxes or construction toys.

Maths Together

The *Maths Together* programme is divided into two sets –
yellow (age 3+) and green (age 5+). There are six books in
each set, helping children learn maths through story,
rhyme, games and puzzles.

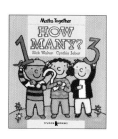

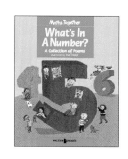

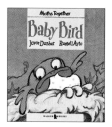

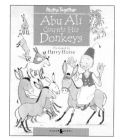